caillou®

Happy Holidays!

Adaptation from the animated film: Marilyn Pleau-Murissi
Illustrations: CINAR Animation, adapted by Éric Sévigny / Coloration: Éric Lehouillier

chouette

COOKIE JAR™

Caillou and Clementine were playing in the snow when Sarah came by.

"Hi Caillou! Hi Clementine! You're invited to the Christmas play at my school."

"Yay! A Christmas play!" exclaimed Caillou. "Is Santa coming soon, Sarah?"

"Pretty soon, Caillou," Sarah answered. "Christmas will be here in two weeks."

When Caillou went home, Mommy was busy at the kitchen table.

"What are you doing, Mommy?"

"I'm writing Christmas cards to send to our friends and family. Would you like to make some too, Caillou?" asked Mommy.

"Yes," Caillou answered. He liked that idea. Caillou worked hard all afternoon making his Christmas cards.

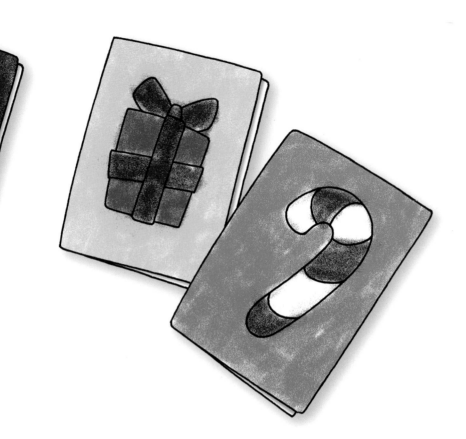

"Daddy, look at all my Christmas cards. Can we give them out tomorrow?" asked Caillou. "We usually mail Christmas cards, Caillou," Daddy answered.

"But they need them before Christmas," Caillou said.

"Don't worry, we'll see that they get them on time," Daddy assured Caillou.

12

"Look, Caillou," Daddy said. "I found something fun to help you keep track of how many days there are until Christmas. It's a calendar that has 12 little windows that open, and there are 12 days left until Christmas. Every night we'll open a window and discover a story behind it."

Caillou loved stories.

"Can we open one now?" he asked.

"Sure," Daddy answered, giving Caillou the calendar.

Caillou gently pulled open the first little window.

"It's a Christmas tree!"

"That's right," Daddy said. "This is a story about the first Christmas tree."

A long time ago, in a faraway place called Germany, there lived a boy named Fritz. His father worked cutting down trees to sell. Sometimes he would take Fritz to work with him. Fritz noticed that at the end of the day the little trees always got left at the bottom of the sled.

Fritz loved trees.
One day he brought a little tree
home for Christmas, because
he thought it would look nice
and smell good.
His mother decorated the tree
to make it prettier.
Since then, many people all
over the world decorate trees
at Christmas.

The next morning, Caillou's daddy had a surprise for the family. They got in the car and drove to Jonah's farm. "Hi Caillou. Hi Rosie," Jonah said. "We're going to go on a sleigh ride to my tree farm in the woods, and you can chose any tree you like."

"A sleigh ride! A Christmas tree farm! Wow!" shouted Caillou.

Caillou and his family went home and got to work
putting up their tree. Daddy got all tangled up in the
lights trying to keep Gilbert away from them.
"Can somebody help me, please," Daddy called out,
giggling.
Everyone was laughing, but soon the lights were strung
and the tree was decorated.

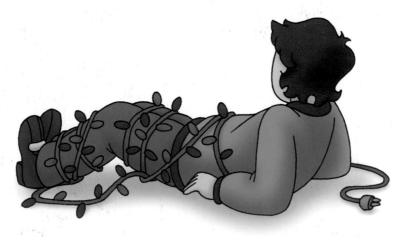

"Can we put my star up now?" Caillou asked.

"Sure can!" replied Daddy.

Once the star was in place, Daddy plugged in the tree lights.

"Wow!" they all exclaimed together.

It was beginning to feel a lot like Christmas now.

"I can't wait to see all the presents under the Christmas tree," said Caillou.

"I know, Caillou," said Mommy. "But Christmas is about more than getting things. Look at all the toys you already have."

"But I don't play with all of them!" Caillou said.

"Maybe you could give some away so someone else can play with them. They would make nice Christmas presents," Mommy said.

11

"How many days are left until Christmas, Caillou?" Mommy asked. Caillou took his calendar and began to count the closed windows, "1, 2, 3, 4, 5, 6, 7, 8, 9, 10, 11!"
"And tomorrow there will be 10," said Mommy.
Caillou opened the next window.

"This story takes place in Mexico," said Mommy. "Several days before Christmas the children of Mexico have a parade. A little boy dresses up as Joseph. And a little girl dresses up as Mary. She rides a donkey. All around them are children dressed up as angels and shepherds."

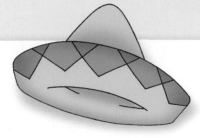

"Following them are three more children dressed up as three wise kings. In Mexico, they speak Spanish. Do you know how they say Merry Christmas? *Feliz Navidad.*"

"*Feliz Navidad,*" repeated Caillou. He loved to learn new words.

The next morning Caillou began to fill a box with toys.
"What Caillou doing?" asked Rosie.
"I'm going to give these toys away so someone else can play with them," answered Caillou.
"You're going to make some children very happy, Caillou," said Mommy.

10

"I hear you were very generous today, Caillou," said Daddy. "Uh-huh," Caillou said proudly. "That's great!" said Daddy. "Are you ready for another story?" Caillou counted the windows, "1, 2, 3, 4, 5, 6, 7, 8, 9, 10!" Opening the next window, Caillou said, "It looks like a school." "It is," answered Daddy.

"A long time ago in a country
called England, some children
were away at school.
They were writing letters to
their families.
The teacher asked them
to decorate their letters to make
them special for Christmas."
"Christmas cards!"
exclaimed Caillou.
"That's right, Caillou. Those
were the first Christmas cards."

"Can we mail my Christmas cards today?" asked Caillou.
"That's a good idea," answered Mommy. "But first, why don't you and Rosie draw a picture for Santa of what you would like for Christmas."
"Horse," Rosie said, as she began to draw.
Caillou said, "I really want a space station!"

Caillou went to Leo's house to play. Leo was painting, and Caillou was making Christmas presents for Rosie and his parents.

"What are you making?" asked Caillou.

"I'm making Hanukkah cards for my parents," answered Leo.

"Is Hanukkah the same as Christmas?" Caillou asked.

"No, we celebrate the Festival of Lights," Leo answered.

Leo's mother called the boys down for some hot chocolate.
"I love hot chocolate!" said Caillou.
Caillou saw a candle holder on the kitchen table and
asked, "What's that?"
"That's a Menorah," answered Leo. "During Hanukkah
we light a candle on the Menorah every night. It lasts
eight days."

It was time to find out what was behind the next window on the calendar. Caillou counted nine, then eight more days to go. Caillou opened the window and asked, "Who's that?"

"That's St. Nick," answered Daddy. "Long ago, in a place called Turkey, there lived a man named Nicholas. He was a kind and generous man. Nicholas felt sorry for a family that lived nearby. They didn't have enough money to buy food."

44

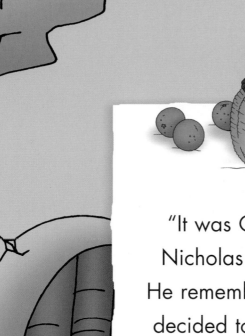
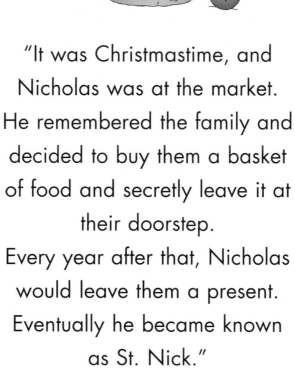

"It was Christmastime, and Nicholas was at the market. He remembered the family and decided to buy them a basket of food and secretly leave it at their doorstep. Every year after that, Nicholas would leave them a present. Eventually he became known as St. Nick."

At Caillou's house, Mommy and
Daddy started to notice that things were missing.
"Have you seen my electric toothbrush?" Daddy asked Mommy.
"No," answered Mommy. "Have you seen my slippers?"
It was a mystery.

While he was waiting for Christmas, Caillou spent
the days playing hockey with Leo, tobogganing, and
learning to ski.
Each night he counted the days, "8, 7, 6."

Caillou's calendar taught him that Santa has many names.
There is *Diet Maros* in Russia. That means Father Frost.

For Christmas in Denmark, *Julemanden* brings surprises.
He plays tricks and wears disguises.

For Christmas in Greece, Santas are called *Killantzaroi*.
They are elves who are full of joy.

52

As Christmas got closer, there were still some mysteries
at Caillou's house. He couldn't find his dinosaur, Rexie,
anywhere.

"Caillou, what are you doing?" asked Mommy.

"I can't find Rexie," answered Caillou.

"I'm sure he'll show up, but right now we need to get
ready to go to the Santa Claus parade!"

Caillou and his family joined the crowds of people in the street. They were waiting for the parade to begin. "Look, Rosie! The majorettes are coming!" said Mommy.

"Santa's elves, too!" Caillou exclaimed.
"Oh, and look who's coming now!"

It was Santa Claus!

"Ho, ho, ho! Merry Christmas!"

"Is Santa going back to the North Pole now, Daddy?"
asked Caillou.

"Not yet. He wants to find out if you've been a good boy,"
answered Daddy. "Let's go see him."
"Yay!" exclaimed Caillou. "Rosie, we're going to see Santa!"

"Santa, I can't find my dinosaur, Rexie," said Caillou.
"Would you like Santa to bring you another dinosaur?"
Santa asked.
"No, there's only one Rexie," said Caillou sadly. "Could
you help me find him?"
"If I see him, I'll put him under your Christmas tree, all
right?" answered Santa.

4

That night it was time for another story.

"A Christmas stocking! It looks like mine!" said Caillou.

"It does!" agreed Daddy.

"Santa's going to fill it with candy, isn't he, Daddy?" asked Caillou.

"I'm sure he will," Daddy answered. "And we'll leave milk and cookies for Santa. Do you know how that tradition started? Boys and girls all over the world would leave things for Santa."

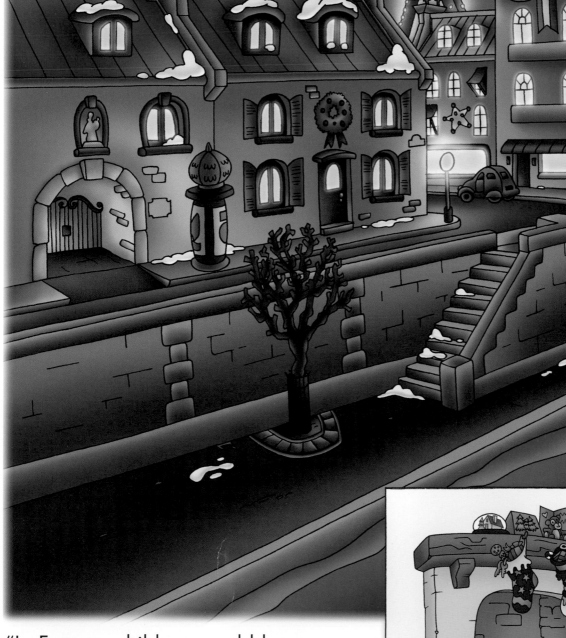

"In France, children would leave their shoes by the fireplace.

In Holland, Santa is called *Sinterklass*, and children there would leave hay and carrots in their shoes for *Sinterklass's* horse.

In Hungary, children would shine their shoes and leave them near the window."

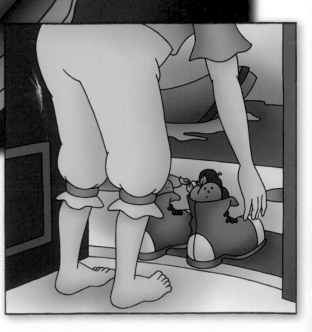

"In Italy, a woman called *La Befana* comes at Christmas. The children there would leave food for her in their shoes outside their front doors.

And in Puerto Rico, the children would leave vegetables under their beds for the camels of the three kings."

The next day, Grandma came over to bake
Christmas cookies with Caillou and Rosie.
They made extra cookies to take to
Grandma's friends at the retirement home.
Caillou gave cookies to everyone.
"I made them myself," he said.
Caillou loved visiting Grandma's friends.
It was like having lots of grandmas and
grandpas.

The time had come for Sarah's play. Caillou and his family got there a bit early while the children were rehearsing their play.

"Caillou!" called Sarah. "We're missing someone."

"Would you take his place in our play?"

"Uh, okay, Sarah." Caillou was nervous at first, but he was
a wonderful snowflake. He said, "It's Christmastime!"

 Caillou was excited. There were only two windows left on his calendar. "Tomorrow is Christmas Eve," said Daddy. "People all over the world eat special things to celebrate Christmas.

In Spain they eat fish called *besugo*,

and they have a roasted duck in Norway.

In France they have
a meal late at night,
called a *reveillon*.

In Austria they eat
cheese pancakes,

and in England
they have
plum pudding."

Caillou's grandma and grandpa arrived, and things got very busy in the kitchen.

Grandma made her apple pie, and Grandpa made the stuffing for the turkey.

Before long, it was time to dress for dinner.
"Why do we have to get dressed up today?" Caillou asked. "Grandma and Grandpa visit us all the time."

"Well, we are celebrating a special night and having a special dinner together," answered Mommy.
Soon they were all sitting at the dinner table, sharing the wonderful food they had prepared together.

It was getting dark outside.

"What do you say if we all go outside and see how our lights look," suggested Grandpa.

So they all dressed up warmly and went outside.

"Ready?" asked Grandpa.

"Ready!"

"Here goes," said Grandpa.

"Wow!" everyone shouted.

When Caillou went to bed, Daddy said,
"Time to open the last window, Caillou."

"It's Santa and his reindeer! Santa's coming!" exclaimed
Caillou. "I'm going to wait up for him."
Daddy whispered, "Santa won't come if you're not asleep.
Sweet dreams, Caillou."

In the morning, Caillou shouted, "It's Christmas!"

"Presents!" Rosie said.

They were beginning to unwrap their presents when Caillou said, "Here's Rexie!"

"Caillou love Rexie," said Rosie.

"Well, look at this!" said Daddy, turning to Mommy. "Your missing slippers."

"Oops," said Mommy. "And here's your electric toothbrush."

They all started to laugh.

"I think Rosie has started a new tradition in our household."

Merry Christmas, everyone!

© 2007 CHOUETTE PUBLISHING (1987) INC. and DHX COOKIE JAR INC.

CAILLOU is a registered trademark of Chouette Publishing (1987) Inc.

Text: adaptation by Marilyn Pleau-Murissi of the animated film Caillou's Holiday Movie,
produced by DHX Media inc.
All rights reserved.
Original screenplay written by Peter Svatek.
Illustrations: Eric Sévigny, based on the animated film Caillou's Holiday Movie
Coloration: Éric Lehouillier
Art Director: Monique Dupras

The PBS KIDS logo is a registered mark of PBS and is used with permission.

We acknowledge the financial support of the Government of Canada through the Canada Book Fund for our publishing activities.

Canadian Patrimoine
Heritage canadien

We acknowledge the support of the Ministry of Culture and Communications of Quebec and SODEC for the publication and promotion of this book.

SODEC
Québec

Bibliothèque et Archives nationales du Québec and Library and Archives Canada cataloguing in publication data

Pleau-Murissi, Marilyn
Caillou: happy holidays!
For children aged 3 and up.
Co-published by: Chouette Publishing Inc. and Cookie Jar Entertainment Inc.

ISBN 978-2-89450-644-8

1. Christmas - Juvenile literature. I. Sévigny, Éric. II. Cookie Jar Entertainment Inc.
III. Title. IV. Title: Happy Holidays!

GT4985.5.P53 2007   j394.2663   C2007-941203-3

Printed in Guangdong, China
10 9 8 7 6 5 4   CHO1886 JUN2013